If You're Not the One

Book Two of the Highland Romance Trilogy

J. Adams

If You're Not the One

A Highland Romance

J. Adams

J. Adams

If You're Not the One

Inveraray Scotland

Drawing strength from Tavish's comforting embrace, I dry my face. I have just spent the last hour on the phone with Audrey, crying empathetic tears, sharing her sorrow. Her news had been bittersweet, but the time for tears has passed and now it's time for action.

"We should get the guest room ready," Tavish murmurs against my brow. "'Twill be a difficult transition for yer sister."

I nod. "Are you really okay with this?"

"Aye. She's family. And we have the room. Question is, are *you* all right with everythin'?"

"Aye," I answer back. "I want ta do everything I can to help her. She needs a new beginning and Inveraray is the perfect place. 'Twas for me. Hopefully she can find the happiness she deserves."

* * *

Salt Lake City, Utah

Audrey Stone is an emotional wreck.

Two months ago, in a moment of loneliness, she made the dumbest decision of her life, and the consequences of that choice are major. She has no excuse. She had been at a low point when she ran into her ex, and had willingly given in to his desires. The next day he was gone.

Now Audrey is pregnant and the baby will never know the father.

Pulling a couple of suitcases from the hall closet, Audrey begins to pack. She hates intruding upon her sister's life, but the offer to have her come and stay with them was too good to pass up and just what Audrey needed. She is excited about starting over somewhere new and is looking forward to seeing Adia again, as well as meeting her husband, but she won't wear out her welcome. She will stay with them just until she can settle into a new life there.

Because now there is more than just herself to think about.

J. Adams

One

Inveraray, Scotland

There are three things I know for certain. One: the earth is an amazing creation. Two: you can find beauty in every part of the highlands. And three: once you step onto Scotland's shores, you never forget the experience because it changes you.

Watching Audrey standing in the backyard with Evan gazing out over the loch, and seeing a new joy radiating from her eyes, the smile gracing her face is a testament of the land's power to change. When Audrey arrived three months ago, she was a wreck and there were many days of tears and pep talks. Her emotions ranged from shame and self-recrimination to anger and hopelessness, and finally, acceptance of the situation. "It is what it is" became her motto. All that was left to do was put her life in God's hands and hope for the best. Tavish and I assured her that she would never be alone and we would help in any way we could.

After some major soul searching, Audrey gained new-found courage and set some goals for herself. After she has the baby she will get a job and move into a small place of her own. She will work to provide a life for her child, keeping her heart closed. She will never allow another man in. That kind of vulnerability would only bring her pain and she refused to allow herself to be hurt again.

But that was before Evan blew into her life.

Evan Mackenzie and Ian MacLeod are Tavish's best friends and two of my favorite people. When Evan came over the first night Audrey was here, he was immediately taken with her and was filled with empathy for her situation. Audrey was cordial to him, but only just, closing herself off from the beginning. But by the end of a month, Evan had pierced her armor, stripping it away piece by painstaking piece and a strong friendship formed between them. It is easy to see that Evan wants more, and I have learned from experience, that, just like Tavish, Evan is a patient man.

I watch Audrey laugh at something Evan says and I smile. She is so petite and small-boned, not even hitting five feet. Her features are even more striking as her smiling eyes meet Evan's. He is ruggedly handsome with his short, red wavy hair, matching beard and mustache, and pale green eyes. The same height and build as Tavish, I joked once that he looks like a giant leprechaun. Evan had simply kissed my cheek, smiled and said he wasn't amused. I baked him a pie to make up. When Audrey playfully made the same comment one day, *he* bake *me* a pie.

"What are ye doing?" Tavish's arms come around me and he presses his hands against my stomach, planting a soft kiss against the side of my neck.

"Just taking in the view."

"So I see," he says, smiling against my cheek. "Ever the matchmaker, ye are."

"I havena said or done anything. Just hoping."

"'Twill happen for them, mark me words."

"And you know this how?" I turn my head, meeting his familiar sly smile.

"Because she's yer sister," he says, kissing me. "She had him charmed the moment they met, just as ye did me. Evan told me how he feels about her. He's a determined man."

As we turn back and continue to watch the two from where we stand on the porch, everything inside me hopes Tavish is right. Audrey deserves to be happy.

* * *

Audrey

Pressing a hands against her stomach, Audrey Stone watches the seagulls swoop down on the loch shore, searching for scraps and skimming the water for small fish. She has always been fascinated with the bird, having spent many a moment observing them back in Utah. Sometimes she finds herself imaging what life is like for them, constantly looking for their next meal, hovering and waiting for a picnicker's leftovers, in some cases even charging in and taking it from a diner's hand. They are definitely determined birds.

Audrey's life has taken a turn she never expected, and she will soon adopt a term she never expected to hear tagged onto her name–single mother. She is thirty-seven years old and pregnant with her first child. It is still hard to grasp at times.

She continues to rub her stomach. Last week she started wearing maternity clothes. Pursing her lips, she ponders the changes her body will continue to go through, feeling certain that it will all be worth it, because she completely loves this baby already. She just wishes that . . . well, there is no sense in wasting time on futile wishes. She just needs to focus her energy on the here and now, on this moment.

"What are ye thinkin' so hard about, lass?" Evan's voice breaks through her pondering.

She smiles at the man whose friendship has come to mean so much to her. "About the future." It wasn't a complete lie.

Evan reaches for her hand. "So am I."

* * *

Evan

Evan Mackenzie is hopelessly in love. He knows Audrey doesn't feel the same, but he can tell she cares for him. For some couples, what he is about to offer has started on less. That's something. But for now, maybe his love would be enough for both of them. Staring into her brown eyes, he is suddenly nervous–more nervous than he has ever been, and for a policeman, that is saying a lot. Gathering his courage, he forges on.

"The babe will need a father and a name." Watching her expression change, he continues. "I love you, Audrey, and I want to marry ye and be a father to yer child."

Audrey sighs. "I care for you, Evan, very much, but I don't love you. And I could never marry you just to give my child a father. I couldn't use you that way." She tries to pull her hand away, but his hold is firm.

"Audrey, just listen to me. You wouldna be using me. I would be getting something out of it, too. I've always been alone. Me Ma and Da died years ago and I dinna have any siblings. 'Tis just me. I'm thirty-five years auld and I'm tired of being alone. I love you and I love this baby. Maybe you will grow to love me one day, but I willna ask of ye anymore than you are willing to give. Just having you with me and being able to take care of ye is enough. You don't even have ta share me bed if you don't want to. Having you there will finally make my house a home."

Evan squeezes her hand, his heart aching at the confusion in her eyes. "Please think on it, lass. Promise me you'll think on it."

Audrey turns away and stares out into the distance, her eyes seeming to fix on something beyond his view. Exhaling a deep breath, she finally nods. "I'll think about it."

J. Adams

Two

The Inveraray Castle has stood on the shores of Loch Fyne since the 1400s. It is the home of the Dukes of Argyll and the seat of Clan Campbell. This is my first visit here, as well as Andrea's, and we are both stunned by the opulence and colors of the interior, which is all hand-painted. From the State Dining room, Tapestry room and Armory Hall (an impressive room by itself with its twenty-one meters high ceiling) on the ground floor, to the Gallery and Clan room on the first floor, every inch of the place is full of splendor and history. There are so many rooms I could get lost easily. Fortunately, Tavish and Evan are very familiar with the castle, which is why after we've toured the entire building, the men leave us to browse in the gift shop while they make their way back to the Armory Hall.

Audrey and I take our time perusing all the items. Much of it is Clan Campbell merchandise. There are food gifts, children's toys, hats, ties and other pieces of clothing. There are also some gorgeous baby clothes and accessories, Scottish produced blankets, greeting cards, and many other things. I pick out a few items for our baby, as well as Audrey's. As usual, she protests, but when I continually ignore her, she finally gives in.

"Evan is in love with me," she tells me as we look at the blankets.

No surprise there, sister. "I know."

"I figured you might."

"Well, 'tis obvious just watching him with you. He doesna attempt to hide it at all."

"Yeah." She pauses. "He asked me to marry him. He wants to take care of me and be a father to the baby."

Though I have hoped and prayed it would happen, the news is still a pleasant surprise. "What did you tell him?"

"I promised him I would think about it. But I

honestly, I don't think I can do it. I care for him. He's a dear friend, but I don't love him. A marriage should start with both people loving each other, and I never wanted to be married again."

"Why is that?"

"You know why, Adia. I can't deal with that kind of hurt again."

I do understand. Her first husband had been a total womanizer and was never faithful. She loved him, but it wasn't enough to hold him. In the end he left, and her trust was shattered. Two years of marriage down the drain–two years of her life that she can never get back.

I lay a hand on my sister's arm. "Evan is not Keith, Audrey. He is a good man who loves ye desperately. If you will allow yerself to, I know you will grow to love him just as much. He is one of the best men I know and he has invited you into his life, something he has never done with anyone else." I squeeze her arm. Accept what he is offering. I believe God has opened this way for ye. He opened a loving man's heart. Take it, Audrey. Take the life that is bein' handed to you."

She looks into my eyes and smiles. "You really are happy, aren't you?"

15

"Aye," I answer, returning her smile. "Moving to Scotland and marrying Tavish is the best thing that has ever happened to me." I rub my stomach. "And having his bairn is another." When she looks down and touches her own stomach, I lay my hand over hers where it rests. "Evan will be good to ye, Audrey. He will do all he can ta make you happy and you will never want for anything."

"And if it doesn't work out?" she challenges, fixing her eyes on mine.

"I believe it will. But don worry. We will always be here for ye. Now, let's go find the men. Tavish promised to treat us ta lunch in the Tearoom. I've heard the quiche and scones are amazing."

* * *

Audrey

Catching up to the men outside the Armory Hall, Audrey touches Evan's arm and he turns to her, his eyes bright and so full of love it makes her heart ache.

"Can I talk to you?"

"Aye," he says, taking her hand and leading her

away from Adia and Tavish. "We'll meet you in the Tearoom," he tells them.

Standing at the end of the hallway, Audrey looks up at him, allowing her gaze to travel over his ruggedly-handsome features. Can she really open up to enough to marry him? Can she trust in his love that much–love that at the moment is unrequited? She has already been hurt not once, but twice, and by the same man. If this doesn't work out . . . No, she can't think like this. She owes it to herself, and Evan, to try.

"You promise not to hurt me?"

Evan's green eyes grow soft and misty. "I promise ye, lass, I willna hurt ye. You will be a part of me and I could not hurt you without hurting meself." He draws her to him, wrapping her in his arms and she closes her eyes, soaking in his embrace. "I'm no perfect, Audrey," he whispers against her brow. "No man is. But I would walk through hell for ye. And as I said before, I willna ask for more than ye can give. Having you with me . . . 'twill be enough."

Releasing a deep sigh and drawing her courage to the surface, she whispers, "I'll marry you."

Three

One Week Later

Audrey and Evan quietly marry in our backyard. The only guests attending besides Tavish and I are Ian MacGregor and a few other close friends that have gotten to know Audrey. Though Evan knows many people in Inveraray, his inner circle is small. How grateful I am that we are included in that circle.

Evan is a handsome groom in a wedding kilt made of the Mackenzie Clan tartan. Audrey is beautiful in a cream-colored, formal maternity dress we found in Glasgow.

The two speak their vows, exchange rings, and are pronounced husband and wife. Then Evan draws her close and kisses her. I smile at the expression on Audrey's face as their lips part. I'm guessing Evan's kiss affected her a lot more than she'd expected it to.

Good for you, Evan!

We have a light lunch before the newlyweds leave for Oban for a week. Since Tavish and I are the only ones aware of the circumstances of their marriage, everyone else assumes it will be a typical honeymoon. I keep hoping something will happen to change things, that Audrey's heart will open enough to embrace the moments of closeness and allow intimacy to happen. In any event, they are married now and that is what's important.

Before they left, Audrey told me she is going to wait until she returns to call Mama and Yvonne. I am sure they will be very disappointed because they have now missed two marriages.

The house is empty now, the last guest leaving a few minutes ago. Standing in the middle of the guestroom, I become lost in thought. All of Audrey's things have been moved to her new home so the room is back to normal. I will miss having my sister with us, but I am happy she and Evan are married and grateful we have our privacy again. Not that her staying with us had been a problem at all. I'm just happy about the way things have worked out.

After we finish putting the food away (we sent a fair amount of it with Audrey and Evan) Tavish suggests that we take a walk. We head down to the shore. Lacing his fingers through mine, we casually stroll along the loch and recap the morning, as well as speculate about the future. It is the first week of August and the weather is humid and very warm, but the temperatures are a lot milder than the scorching heat I was used to during August in Utah.

"How are you feeling?" Tavish asks me.

"Big."

He laughs, kissing my hand. "Ye're lovely."

"Thank you." I squeeze his hand in return. "I'm glad you love me regardless of my size."

"Always, love."

Gazing at his profile as he looks ahead and taking in his smiling expression, I again count myself the luckiest woman in the world. Tavish is an amazing husband. I want for nothing, and if it is in his power to give, he gives it. He loves with all that he is and holds nothing back. Every day and moment with him is a joy, and I never tire of being near him.

I stop for a moment and flex my left leg. The prosthetic foot is rubbing a little, probably from standing so much today, especially with the extra weight of the pregnancy. Tavish's concern is immediate. It always is when it comes to my discomfort in any way.

"Is it bothering ye, love?"

"A little. I think I'm just a little tired."

"You've been exhausted a lot lately. Let's head back," he says, turning us around. He wraps an arm around my waist, drawing me against his side. "I'll rub it for ye and you can nap for a while."

I smile. "Thanks for always takin' care of me."

"Ye're welcome."

* * *

Audrey

The small resort town of Oban is known as the seafood capital of Scotland. It is beautiful and Audrey falls in love with it immediately. Evan told her he spent a lot of time there as a boy, watching the fishing boats come in to unload their daily catch, and it was a special place for him. That is why he wanted to bring her there. He is looking forward to showing her around.

The small lochside rental home they will be staying in is charming and cozy. The interior is light and airy with a country Scottish feel. There are two large, tastefully decorated bedrooms, each with a private bathroom.

Standing in the hallway, Evan asks, "Which room would you like?" His smile is easy, but Audrey can see him working hard to mask the longing he carries inside. She has come to know him that well.

"I'll take this one, if it's okay," she answers, gesturing to the one on the right. It has a beautiful view of the lake.

"'Tis verra okay. I thought ye would want that one because of the view." He places her bag on the bed. "Are ye tired? You can rest up a bit if you are."

"I'm okay. I'll just take a moment to put my things away. I would love to sit out on the deck."

"Sounds good. I'll leave ye to it and go and put the food away. I'll meet you outside." He smiles and leaves her to unpack.

Audrey puts her clothes in the dresser drawers and places her cosmetic and toiletry case on the bathroom counter.

Sitting on the bed, Audrey contemplates that she is now Mrs. Evan Mackenzie. She had never planned to marry again. It hadn't been in the cards for her and she had accepted that. But it seems fate had another deck stashed away and chose to deal the hand when she'd least expected it. The long ago faded dream of having a family of her own has now been granted. But she always assumed love would be what brought it to her.

Still, as she ponders her situation, she realizes there are far worse things than marrying a friend. Shaking off these thoughts, she heads out to join Evan on the deck. She finds him staring out over the loch. When she approaches, he smiles and slides over on the cushioned bench, making room for her.

For a while they don't speak, they simply soak in the soothing sound of the water lapping against the shore. Evan's arm is draped across the back of the bench, his warmth brushing against her. Audrey glances at his profile. He looks relaxed and happy. She wonders how he can be happy marrying a woman who doesn't love him. She also wonders how long he will be content with things the way they are between them. Closing her eyes, she shakes her head slightly, dislodging the thought. She won't allow herself to dwell on it now.

"Thank you, Evan. It was a lovely wedding."

He turns to her. "No need ta thank me, lass. I should be thanking you for marrying me. Thank you for bein' my wife. You've made me verra happy." He reaches for her hand.

Choosing not to doubt his feelings, Audrey laces her fingers through his. It is an intimate gesture, but she takes comfort in knowing that he won't ask for more. And thinking back on the way his kiss had affected her, she wonders if she would even be able to stop herself from giving in to physical intimacy if he pushed it.

But she doesn't want that. At least not right now.

* * *

Evan

A deep sense of contentment washes over Evan as he and Audrey hold hands and take this moment to just be. She is his now and he takes comfort in that knowledge. Yes, he wants a complete marriage and desires to share every intimacy with her, but he will not break his word by trying to push her into something she isn't ready for. He will simply love her and be patient. When she is finally ready for the next step, she will let him know.

By choice, Evan has not been with a woman in years. Though he had grown to want more than physical pleasure, he had never really desired to have something deeper with anyone until Audrey. Simply put, he has come to love Audrey more than anything. And marrying her–even if it's just in name only–was worth it.

She is worth the wait.

Four

Last night I called my midwife, Ginny, and talked with her about the exhaustion and discomfort I've been feeling. She came over to examine me and gave us some news that we are still trying to digest. She found a second heartbeat.

I am just two months away from my due date and she found a second heartbeat!

We are having twins!

Hearing the news, I went from laughing to crying to laughing again. And of course, Tavish was beside himself with joy.

Early this morning we went to Ginny's birthing

center for an ultrasound. We are having a girl and a boy. Per Ginny's orders, I will rest today, which means my shopping trip is off, but since we will now be buying for two, I'll just order everything online.

Two babies. I am still trying to wrap my head around it. I suddenly feel inadequate, and I hope I can handle everything. Tavish assures me that he will always be there to help. I am even more grateful now that he works from home.

Tavish enters the family room with a glass of ice water and my laptop. He places the water on the table and hands me the computer before sitting next to me on the sofa and draping my legs over his lap.

"Ready ta shop?" he asks.

I smile, drawing on our mutual joy, pushing away any and all negativity. I can handle this. I can handle anything. "I'm always ready to shop."

I won't worry anymore. I will simply concentrate on being ready for motherhood. These babies are a blessing and a gift. I silently thank God for them and have faith that all will be well.

* * *

Audrey

After quickly eating breakfast, Audrey and Evan get an early start on sightseeing.

Because Evan knows how much Audrey enjoys exploring old church's, cathedrals and castles, they start at Dunstaffnage Castle and Chapel. Once the stronghold of Clan MacDougall, the castle sits on the edge of the loch. It was captured by Robert the Bruce in 1309 and remained in his possession for several years. The castle was used to fight off Vikings and the massive curtain wall is one of the oldest standing castle remains in Scotland. The chapel is tucked away amongst the trees, part of it having been converted to a family graveyard.

The castle stairs are a little difficult to walk up and Evan holds tightly to Audrey's hand. When they reach the top, Audrey decides the climb was worth it because the view is spectacular.

"This is incredible!" she says, looking out over the green valley.

"I knew ye would love it."

"Oh, I do."

"You have a thing for castles. I knew the moment ye laid eyes on Inveraray Castle."

"There's just something so alluring about them. Like many little girls, I used to dream that I would one day be swept up by a handsome prince and taken to his castle to live."

Evan's smile is thoughtful as he stands next to her, taking in the view. "Well, I'm no prince and the home I offer ye is no palace, but if 'twere in my power, I would give ye a grand palace."

Hearing the grave tone of his voice, Audrey touches his arm, drawing forth a smile. "I know, but your home is lovely, and it's enough for me."

"*Our* home," he says, covering her hand.

She smiles again. "Our home."

They visit the small information room with a model of the castle built the way it once was. Audrey asks plenty of questions, getting a history lesson to add to her growing Scottish knowledge. She thoroughly enjoys the visit.

Next, they visited the Dunollie House, another MacDougall owned castle. They enter the maid's house and are given a little history about the castle. There are a few displays set up, detailing the life of servants back then, and there is a historic naval display on the top floor. The castle itself is just a ruin and there isn't much of it left. Evan helps Audrey up the steep muddy hill to get to the ruin. They reach the castle to find only four walls and a cross monument. Though this castle isn't as exciting as Dunstaffnage, Audrey is still glad she got to see it.

They visit Purdie's Scottish Soap Factory where Audrey immerses herself in smelling the different scents. She has never seen such an amazing assortment of natural products. Evan purchases some Scotland-made scented candles, soaps, lotions and several scents of body wash for her. In fact, he adds shampoos, conditioners, and Scottish chocolates, and has a large basket made up for her. Audrey kisses his cheek and thanks him, looking forward to pampering herself with the products.

They stop by a quaint little pub for lunch and have fish and chips. Audrey declares they are the best she has ever tasted. After lunch, they stop by the store for a few more groceries, then head back to their place. Audrey again thanks Evan for the wonderful day.

"Ye're welcome, love. I'm glad for the opportunity to show ye around a place that means so much to me. I love coming because of the memories of the days I spent here with me da."

"It meant a lot to me that we came."

They stood looking at each other, both at a loss of what else to say. Audrey hates these moments because they are so awkward. She knows it is partly her fault. True, Evan knew what he was getting into by marrying her, but she'd never stopped to think about just how hard it would be to deprive him of emotions and actions he should be able to freely express as a newlywed. It hurts her heart to see him trying so hard to act normal and unaffected.

"Ye're tired," he finally says. "Maybe you should rest for a bit."

"I am a little tired," she agrees. "I think I'll lay down for a while."

* * *

Evan

He smiles as she walks away, the upward curve of

his mouth fading when he hears her room door close. Pressing a hand to his heart, he closes his eyes, willing the ache away. Evan wants his wife with ever fiber of his being. He needs her with an intensity that makes tears press, but he refuses to let them come. And he refuses to push her. He'd promised her that, and he has never been a man to break promises.

Exiting the house through the patio doors, Evan stares out into the distance for a moment before walking down the long path stretching through a garden area down to the shore. On the side of the loch is a sitting area with patio furniture. It is a somewhat secluded spot, offering a little privacy. Sitting on the bench, he ponders his many blessings, refusing to let another sad thought enter his mind. He is healthy and strong. He has a good job with steady pay, a nice home, and now he has a gorgeous wife and a bairn on the way. He is finally going to be a father. Life has been very good to him.

Evan stares out over the loch for so long, he loses track of time, and before he realizes it, two hours have past. Audrey is probably awake.

As he gets up to go back inside, he sees her walking

down to him, and the look in her eyes makes every other thought fade from his mind.

* * *

Audrey

Audrey's sleep had been filled with disjointed dreams–dreams of Utah and her mother and Yvonne. Dreams of sailing down Loch Fyne on a small boat completely alone, and then reaching land, realizing it was actually the sandy shore of the Great Salt Lake. And finally, dreams of Evan, of his smile, his laugh, and the kiss he gave her at the wedding. She relived that moment over and over at the end of each dream.

The dreams have produced a hunger inside her, a burning need to be touched and loved. A hunger for *his* touch.

Now, as she approaches him, an emotional war wages within her–a war between her head and the desires of the body. Then his eyes meet hers, and the hunger wins. When she reaches him, her cheeks warm as his gaze roams over her face. In his green eyes she sees his own burning passion, so carefully reined in–

passion that she knows is only waiting for her permission to roll forth.

"I . . . need you," she finally whispers. "Will you . . ."

"Aye," he breathes. His warm mouth is immediately feasting upon hers, his muscular arms enfolding her and pressing her body against his.

It is a mutual consent of emotions and physical yearning speaking to one another, a language understood by both, with no need of another uttered word.

Five

Audrey

Audrey and Evan get dressed and have a late dinner. Staring at one another across the table, a new heat rushes through her as memories of the intimacy they shared fill her mind. His love for her was clear, for he had whispered of that love with each caress of his hands and each kiss on her lips, her skin. She can also see the love shining through his eyes, feel the warmth of his adoring gaze as it roams over her face.

And she likes the way it makes her feel, the way *he* is making her feel. Even though her feelings are not as strong, she does care, and he *is* her husband. Why shouldn't she enjoy being loved by him?

It had been nice lying in Evan's arms afterward, just holding one another. She had never experienced that part of intimacy before. Her ex had always used her and quickly gotten up and dressed, moving on to other things. He hadn't been the holding type . . .

Stop it! She must stop going back. Keith doesn't deserve a place in her thoughts. He never did. Besides, she is married to a good man now. Adia is right. Evan is not Keith. He is nothing like Keith. Hasn't he proved that already?

Even with this knowledge, part of Audrey still cannot completely let him in. She wants to, but the gate her heart is locked behind needs a crowbar to open it completely. Maybe Evan has it. Only time will tell. For now, she will work on loosening the bars herself and hope for progress, even if it's a little at a time. She smiles at him. Evan is definitely the kindest man she has ever known. He gives so much of himself and never asks for anything. He simply gives.

* * *

Evan

Evan takes Audrey's hand in his. He has just experienced heaven in her arms, and he wishes they could have stayed in bed even longer than they had. He longs to hold her warm body against him again and prays that since they have crossed this bridge, she will allow him to share her room now and not turn him away to sleep alone.

When Audrey had walked out to him and initiated their intimacy with her soft-spoken "I need you," joyous hope swelled within him. Then he'd kissed her and everything fell into place. For Evan, there is no going back now. He can't.

"So what would ye like ta do tomorrow?" he asks, squeezing her hand.

"It would be fun to visit the Sea Life Sanctuary, maybe go for a walk along the shore."

"That sounds grand. Would ye like to get an early start again?"

"No, I want to sleep in a while, if that's okay."

"Aye, 'tis okay." He hopes his husky voice doesn't betray the longing he feels to sleep in next to her. He clears his throat, charting the course of his thoughts to safer waters. "When we get back home, 'tis okay if ye want to do a little redecorating. The place really could use a feminine touch."

"I love it already," she says, smiling. "It's the perfect size and it's cozy, and the elevated view of Loch Fyne is lovely. I don't want to change anything, maybe just add a few things here and there."

"It's your home now, love. Ye do with it what you wish."

"That involves a little shopping, you know."

"Me wallet is yers."

She laughs. "Thank you. I'm pretty good at bargain shopping. I spent a lot of time at yard sales back in the states. Every Saturday during the summer I would peruse the more prominent neighborhoods and find some great stuff. As they say, one man's trash is another man's treasure."

"Aye. Especially if the treasures are barely used and unnecessarily cast off for somethin' newer."

"Exactly."

"There is a charity shop in Glasgow that sells some nice used furnishings and trinkets. I will have ta take ye there."

"I look forward to it."

Audrey takes her plate over to the sink and rinses it off before putting in the dishwasher. She and Evan clear the table and put everything away.

Suddenly at a loss for words, Evan walks over and stares through the patio doors. The last of daylight is fading away. He watches Audrey's approaching reflection in the glass, feels her warmth without even touching her.

"Tell me what you are thinking, Evan."

"Truthfully?"

"Yes."

He exhales softly, wondering if his honesty will be too much. "I don't want ta sleep alone anymore," he says without turning around. Nothing is said for a moment and he is surprised to feel her hand take his. He finally turns, gazing down at her upturned face. Her words are soft when she replies.

"Neither do I."

Six

When Audrey and Evan come back from their honeymoon, I notice the change in their relationship immediately. The signs of a new level of intimacy between them are obvious. Audrey looks happier and is more accepting of his affection, and Evan's love for her shines even brighter. He has the look of a man who is more content–not completely, but I am sure what he feels for her will be enough to bridge the small gap and guide his wife's heart home.

That evening, Audrey tells me she called Mama and Yvonne and told them she was married, and just as we knew would be the case, they were upset that they hadn't been here. After talking with them for a while,

Audrey managed to calm them down. And according to Audrey, once Evan got on the phone and spoke to them with that sexy Scottish accent of his, things were smoothed over fairly quickly. His offer to pay for them to come for a visit cinched the deal. It seems Evan's gift of persuasion is just as good as Tavish's.

The next day, Audrey and Evan stop by to see us on their way to Glasgow to do a little shopping for house things. She and I sit and visit in the backyard for a few moments. Smiling, she places her hand on my stomach, still unable to get over our surprise news of twins. I am still adjusting to it, myself.

As we take in the view, Audrey shares the details of their honeymoon and how much she enjoyed herself. She tells me about Evan almost buying out Purdie's Scottish Soap Factory for her. I love that store as well. After the kidnapping ordeal, Tavish had had a large basket of products delivered to me and I still pamper myself daily.

"I love Oban," she said. "I love Scotland period. Evan promised to take me to visit more little towns soon. He wants so much to make me happy, and he does. I guess he even asked Tavish to make a couple of

Mackenzie tartan baby blankets. He wants to get the nursery finished soon. He's taking this fatherhood thing seriously." Her smile looks wishful.

"Evan is a good man," I say softly. "He loves ye madly, and whether you believe it or not, you're falling in love with him."

"He's a very good man, but I don't know if it's possible for me to really love him, not like he deserves anyway."

"And why do you think that?"

She sighs. "That's just the way it is. Yes, we're married and I am happy, but . . . it is what it is. However, I did promise myself I would try."

"You don't have to *try* to fall in love, Audrey, it just happens."

"For normal people, yeah," Audrey murmurs.

I laugh, amused by her idea of 'normal people.' "Just take it one day at a time." When she says nothing else, I smile.

Oh, you're getting there, sister. You may not see it, but you're closer than you think.

* * *

After Audrey and Evan leave, Tavish joins me outside. The day is mild and too nice to go back inside.

"Yer sister seems happy," Tavish says, wrapping an arm around me. I rest my head against his shoulder and close my eyes against a slight headache that is slowly building. Tavish went to the store earlier this morning and bought me some Tylenol. It started wearing off a little while ago and I don't want to take more until later.

"She *is* happy. I also think she's falling in love with Evan. She just canna see it yet."

"Aye. I agree. Evan said he longs ta hear her finally say the words, but for now, what they have is enough." He buries a hand in my hair, gently massaging my scalp. I love it when he does that. "Still . . . 'twould be hard, the waiting ta hear it. A man needs to know the heart of his woman."

Lifting my head slightly, I draw his down, meeting his lips with mine. "You will always know yer woman's heart," I whisper.

"Aye," he breathes against my mouth. "Yer heart beats for me, and mine for you. I love ye, darlin'."

"I love you."

I lay my head on his shoulder again and he continues to massage my scalp, his long fingers stretching across the crown. "Is it helping any, love?"

"Some. Maybe I'll lay down for a bit and see if that helps."

"Come on," he says, standing and helping me up, immediately lifting me in his arms.

"I can walk, you know."

"I know ye can."

"But carrying me makes ye feel more manly, right?"

Arching a brow, he smiles slyly. "I ken I'm man enough without needing ta prove meself."

"Don't I know it. After all, 'twas yer manliness that put me in this situation."

He snorts. "And I'll gladly take the credit." He carries me upstairs and places me on the bed, grabbing a light tartan throw to cover my feet. "You get some rest, love," he says, leaning down and kissing me.

I smile and turn to my side, quickly drifting to sleep.

Seven

Audrey

Glasgow is the largest city in Scotland and the third biggest in the United Kingdom. Audrey muses that it is about half the size of Salt Lake City, but with a population of over 595,000, it *is* big for Scotland. Glasgow is a milder area and the August temperatures are a little cooler. As usual, the skies are overcast, making Audrey grateful she brought a sweater. With it still being tourist season, the streets are crawling with people, especially in West End. The area is a bohemian district, full of tea rooms, cafes, boutiques, hotels, and restaurants.

While in West End, Audrey and Evan take a little

stroll through Glasgow Botanic Gardens. It is huge and there are several glasshouses (called greenhouses in America) the main one called the Kibble Palace. The various flowers, trees and tropical plants are beautiful, and Audrey takes many pictures with her phone. Evan then asks a passing tourist to take a picture of them together.

They stop at a cafe to have some lunch. Sitting at a table by the window, Evan watches people going to and fro and Audrey finds herself watching him. She is definitely married to a handsome man. He is kind, giving and loving, putting her needs, feelings and desires before anything or anyone else's, including his own. He is so perfect for her, it's unbelievable at times. She just wishes she could be the same for him. She continues to stare at his profile. When he turns and smiles at her adoringly with those twinkling green eyes, she decides that she will try her very best to be those things for him, to be the wife he deserves. He takes her hand in his and she smiles.

The server soon delivers their order of shrimp salad croissant sandwiches with homemade chips and a side of Waldorf salad. They leisurely enjoy their lunch, warm conversation flowing between them.

Afterward, they head to the charity shop. Opening the door for her, Evan says again, "My wallet is yers, darlin'."

She grins. "I promise not to break the bank. I'm a bargain shopper, remember?"

"Aye, and I'm ready ta watch your skills at work."

Perusing the store, Audrey finds a crystal vase and tartan place mats for the dining room table, a cozy throw to drape on the family room sofa, a Scottish doll in a kilt for the fireplace mantle. She finds a framed print of Inveraray Castle, a Scottish cookbook–which will definitely come in handy–a silk fern for the living room, and a set of porcelain china decorated in red roses. She also picks out a couple of accent tables, a decorative trunk, and a lovely beige glider rocker for the baby's room.

"I think I'm done now," Audrey says.

"Are ye sure? I think there is still room in the truck for a kitchen sink."

"Ha ha," she says, poking him and he laughs. They head to the register.

* * *

Evan

I love this woman so much, God. My heart aches with love for her.

Evan stares down at Audrey while they wait for their purchases to be rung up. He is grateful for the time they have spent together shopping, but he longs to be home alone with her and have her in his arms again. When he'd caught her staring at him during lunch, his heart had leaped and he knew God was working on hers. He hadn't wanted to ruin the moment with words. He had simply smiled and hoped she could read the love in his expression.

"Wow!" he says, surprised by the total. His wife really is a bargain shopper. He had planned to spend much more. "Did ye want to go by another shop?" he asks as they carry everything out to the truck.

"Nope, I think I'm good. There were a few things I saw at a shop in Inveraray that I would like to get if it's okay."

"Completely. Buy anything you want."

"Thank you, Evan." She kisses his cheek.

"Ye're welcome, love. Any time."

Eight

Tavish

While Adia takes a late afternoon nap, Tavish gets some more work done. A friend placed another order last week for some tartan items to sell in his gift shop and Tavish has been finishing up the last of it. Afterward, he heads to the kitchen and makes dinner for his wife, then takes a tray up to her. He quietly sets it on the table and sits down on the bed beside her, watching her sleep. She is so beautiful, like a princess, and he never tires of looking at her. Unable to help it, he leans over and kisses her.

Adia awakens, smiling dreamily. "Mmmm, I'm

about ta be a little corny here. Sigh, my prince has finally come."

He laughs. "We havena even been married a year and we're already thinking alike."

"I know. Just imagine what we'll be like fifty years from now. I'll probably have ta walk around with me head wrapped in aluminum foil to keep you from reading my thoughts. I'm sure I will be pretty ornery by then."

"Och, don't you worry none. I'll ken just what to do to take care of yer ornery disposition." He kisses her again with a strong trace of passion."

"Then I'll always have something to look forward to," she breathes.

"Aye." His voice is raspy. "I'm going to deliver an order, but I'll tend to ye when I get back."

She smiles. "I'll be here."

* * *

How I love that man.

I eat the dinner Tavish prepared, more grateful for him than I can possibly say. I couldn't ask for a more loving or attentive husband. He makes each new day better than the one before and I can't imagine not having him in my life.

After finishing, I place the plate on the table and get up and walk across the hall to the nursery. We finished decorating it last month. The walls are painted light blue with sea green baseboards and crown molding. The crib and dresser are cherry wood, the bedding green, white, and yellow polka dots, as well as the curtains. A yellow glider rocker sits in the corner and a large, beige plush area rug covers the hardwood floor. Tavish had gone on a stuffed animal shopping spree and there are large bears and other animals in various colors sitting in every corner of the room.

I smile, taking in the beautiful room. Every day we take a moment to stand in the doorway of the nursery and gaze about the room, imagining what it will be like to have our baby-correction, babies-there. I glance at the wooden plaque Tavish made just this morning with our babies' names engraved on it: Gavin and Ainsley. Their names are surround by an etched tartan pattern. I had no idea Tavish was so gifted in woodwork. He constantly amazes me. When I asked him why he never told me, he said he likes surprising me.

Smiling at the memory, I return to our room and sit on the small sofa, propping my feet up on the ottoman, and continue working on a poem I started before my nap, pausing a moment to gaze through the window at the view that inspires my rambling thoughts about nature.

Sometimes I wonder why we don't listen.

We have ears, yet we do not use them.

Why do we misuse what has been gifted to us?

We close our senses, embracing hearts that have grown cold with time,

missing the beating heart beneath us,

And the land cries.

Wars have laid waste upon the shores,

history is doomed to repeat itself.

Mother Earth moans, voicing in questioning supplication, "Will they never learn?"

Her tears of thunder crash upon the rocks,

the drops striking and cleansing with urgency.

The day of retribution is drawing near, yet not near enough,

And still, the land cries.

I pause a moment, giving my mind time to process the thoughts churning in the creative part of my brain, but the ringing of the doorbell quickly draws me from my musings. I hurry down to answer it, surprised to find Audrey standing there with tears in her eyes, making me wonder if her day with Evan in Glasgow was a total bust.

"What is it?" I ask, drawing my sister inside.

"I need to talk."

J. Adams

Nine

Audrey

Audrey sits on the sofa with her legs tucked under her and Adia sits next to her, concern wrinkling her brow.

"What's going on?"

"I don't know."

"What do ye mean you don't know?"

"I mean I don't know!" Audrey releases a frustrated breath, wishing she could explain what is going on inside her.

"Ye're lying, Audrey." When Audrey opens her mouth to protest, Adia cuts her off. "Did everything go okay with your trip today?"

Audrey nodded, looking away. "Everything was fine. Great actually."

"Did Evan do or say something to upset you?"

"No. Evan would never hurt me."

"Are you feeling okay, health-wise?"

"I feel fine." Audrey glances at her sister, seeing the frustration in her eyes.

"You're not giving me much help here. If everything is okay and you two didna have an argument or anything, what's wrong?"

Audrey shakes her head as tears fill her eyes. "I don't understand what my problem is. I just had an amazing day and I'm angry."

"Why are you angry?"

"I don't know!"

Adia sighs, pausing a moment before speaking again. "Audrey, I don't completely understand what's happening here, but one thing is obvious. Ye're falling in love with your husband and you are fighting it."

"I'm not –"

"You *are*. Why do you deny it? Why do you keep fighting it? That man adores you and worships the ground you walk on. Why won't ye admit to yourself that you're in love with him and open your heart?"

Tears fall down her face and before she can stop herself, she blurts, "Because I don't want to be hurt, that's why!"

Adia's voice is soft. "How can you think that when you just told me you know Evan would never hurt you?"

"I don't know." Audrey's mind and heart is filled with confusion, her fear at war with her feelings for Evan–feelings she can no longer deny, no matter how hard she tries. She hadn't wanted this. She hadn't wanted to fall in love. Love is too complicated and puts her heart in a vulnerable and unsafe position. She thought she was doing so well keeping her emotions in the 'caring' mode and figured that wouldn't change for a long while yet, but today when they had arrived home, Evan had taken her in his arms and kissed her, murmuring over and over, "I love ye, my own." He'd immediately carried her to their room and made such perfect love to her, she hadn't wanted to let him go. She had suddenly felt the burning need to be in his arms forever. That was when something cracked inside her and the fissures began to slowly grow. She'd immediately gotten up and said she needed to see her sister, turning away from the confused and hurt look on his face. Quickly getting dressed, she'd jumped in the truck and rushed over to Adia's.

And now here she sits, having tried to run away from feelings that only followed her here.

"Audrey, Evan is a good man. Go home and talk ta him."

"I can't," she says, shaking her head.

"Why?"

"I just can't. Not now. Not yet."

Adia sighes. "All right, I willna push you. Just sit here a while. I'll go and make us some tea."

"Thank you," Audrey says, sniffling.

* * *

After putting the kettle on, I dial Tavish's number and speak softly so Audrey can't hear me.

"Hello, love," comes his beloved voice.

"Hi. Audrey is here and not doing too well. Would ye go and see Evan? I think he might need ta talk."

Not hesitating, he answers, "Aye. I'm on my way."

Hanging up the phone, I close my eyes and say a prayer for Audrey and Evan. I know they are both in God's hands, and somehow everything will work out.

J. Adams

Ten

Evan

"Talk to her, man."

"I will."

Walking to the door, Evan hugs Tavish and thanks him for coming by. Tavish had given him a lot to think about and he is grateful for his friend's insight. Evan ponders their visit.

When Tavish had arrived, he had sat down at the table while Evan pulled a pan of leftover cobbler and a jug of milk from the fridge.

"Adia send you over?"

"Aye."

Grabbing some plates from the cabinet, Evan dished out

the cobbler and poured two glasses of milk.

The men ate in comfortable silence. After a while Tavish said, "Talk to me."

Evan sighed. "I dinna ken how to reach her. Every time I think I'm getting closer to her heart, she pulls away."

"She's scared, Evan. And I think this goes beyond the trust issue. I wonder if a large part of the problem is Audrey thinking she doesna deserve ta be happy, that she doesn't deserve you. Maybe because of the way her ex abandoned her—not just once but twice—deep down, she feels she's no good enough."

"She couldna be more wrong."

"Tell her that. Help her ta believe it. When she finally starts to believe it, she will open her heart to ye. Whether she wants to admit it or not, she loves ye."

Now, as Evan thinks back on Tavish's words, he feels there is a lot of truth in what he said. He just needs to figure out how to reach Audrey.

Please, help me ta reach her, Lord. She's everything to me.

* * *

It is dark when Audrey gets back. Evan has been sitting in the living room waiting for her and praying for guidance. He stands and approaches her, noticing her red eyes immediately. "Can we talk, love?"

"I'm tired." She turns to go upstairs, but he stops her.

"Audrey, please dinna turn away from me." When she heaves a resigned sigh, he forges on. "I love you, Audrey, so much that I ache inside. I've loved ye from the first moment I saw ye." He softly touches her face, brushing away the tears trailing down her cheeks. "I dinna ken what's going on inside you, but I know you care for me, Audrey." She's says nothing, she just averts her eyes, looking at everything but him. "Please say something."

She covers her face and turns away. Drawing nearer, he wraps his arms around her, holding her close. He can feel her trembling.

* * *

Audrey

"Please talk to me, love," Evan pleads. "Open yer

heart to me."

Audrey closes her eyes, soaking in his warmth, her head urging her to push him away, but her heart unearthing buried words, pushing them to the surface. And she is so weary of fighting. She finally turns to face him, gripping his arms where the ivory linen shirt stretches over his biceps, the tails no longer tucked inside his kilt.

"I care for you more than I can say, Evan. I love you. I never thought I could love someone so much." She released a frustrated breath, pulling away. "But it doesn't matter."

"What do you mean it doesn't matter? How could it not?"

Unwilling to answer him, she heads upstairs, hoping he won't follow her, but knowing he will. As soon as she reaches their room, he enters right behind her.

"Talk to me, Audrey. How could you loving me not matter? 'Tis all I've ever wanted."

"It doesn't matter!"

"Why? Tell me why!"

"Because love is never enough! Because I'm not

enough! And one day you will realize that. When you finally do, it will be too late for me, because you will toss that love away. I couldn't handle that, Evan! I couldn't!" Broken, she sits on the edge of the bed and sobs.

Evan kneels down in front of her. "Oh, *mo ghraidh*, I could never do that to ye. Do you hear me? Never!" The vehemence in his voice draws her eyes to his. He takes her hand and presses it against his heart. "Ye feel that, love? Me heart is yers. It's beating for you and no one else. You're enough for me Audrey. You're more than enough, and you always will be. Throwing your love away would be throwing away a gift from God. 'Twould be throwing away me own life's breath. I could not survive without it. It's not possible for me to live without yer love now. No, my lass, you are more than enough. You deserve ta be happy, and til my dying breath, I will live to make you happy."

Staring into his eyes, she can hardly breathe. Releasing her hand, Evan takes her face between his palms and crushes his mouth to hers, his kiss voracious in its passion. Sliding her arms around his neck, tears slip down her cheeks as he ravenously feasts upon her and she returns his kiss with equal intensity, every part of her turning to liquid in his arms. His embrace is heaven, his kiss stirring her emotions so much, she finally parts her lips from his and presses her face against his shoulder. She is still trembling, but for a different reason now. She loves him. With every fiber of her being she loves him. She couldn't deny it now if she tried.

"Give me yer heart," he whispers against her ear. "Give me your heart and I'll protect it with all that I am."

Drawing back, she looks into his eyes and whispers, "You have it."

With tears falling down his face, Evan pulls her down into his lap and cradles her in his arms, rocking her slowly. He begins to softly hum, then quietly sing, his voice low and deep.

Cailin mo rùin-sa is leannan mo ghràidh,
Ainnir mo chridh-sa 's i cuspair mo dhàin.
Tha m'inntinn làn sòlais bhi tilleadh gun dàil,
Gu cailin mo rùin-sa is leannan mo gràidh.

B'òg chuir mi eòlas air leannan mo ghràidh,

'S a rinn mise suas ri'sa ghleannan gu h-àrd;
A gnuis tha cho aoidheil, làn gean agus bàigh,
Is mise bhios cianail, mur faigh mi a làmh.

"What is that?" Audrey asks.

"It's called "Dearest My Own One." 'Tis an old Gaelic love song."

"It sounds beautiful."

"I can sing it in English if ye'd like."

"I would." She smiles as he tightens his embrace and continues.

Dearest my own one, oh won't you be mine,
Full of devotion, so modest and kind?
My heart's full of longing and yearning for you;
Come close to me, darling --- you know I'll be true.

How charming you were, dear, when first in the glen
I made your acquaintance, and ever since then
Without you I'm lonely; none other will do;
Those brown eyes enthralled me --- it had to be you.

Do you remember that moment of bliss,
So fondly embracing, the thrill of that kiss?

Since then you are mine, dear, the choice of my heart;
My promise I'll give you, that we'll never part.

"I love it," she tells him.

"I'm glad." He gently tips her chin up, looking down into her eyes a moment before brushing his lips against hers and whispering, "I love ye, dearest my own one."

Audrey smiles as warmth fills her–warmth and security that she knows she can only find with him. She truly is his own one. And she is finally content with that.

"I love you, Evan."

Epilogue

Two years later

Tavish and I laugh as my sister, Yvonne, and Ian chase Gavin and Ainsley around the yard. My sister and mother have been visiting for the last two weeks and are leaving tomorrow. This was their second trip to Scotland and they've fallen in love with it all over again. Today we've been having a barbeque for them. I will definitely miss them, and I have talked to Tavish about taking a trip to the states. We're planning to go for Christmas.

Smiling, I wave to Mama where she sits on the porch swing with Tavish's father, the two of them watching their posterity.

As I watch our two little ones play, I see so much of their father in them. Both have dark auburn hair and hazel eyes. Already, it is apparent that Gavin will inherit Tavish's height and size. Not yet two, he is a tall toddler. Ainsley, however, has inherited the petite gene from my side of the family. She is even smaller than Evan and Audrey's little Sarah, named after our mother.

Gavin shoots around Ian's legs, chasing his sister. I can't believe how fast Ainsley is and I'm worn out just watching them. My husband wraps his arms around me, sweeping my hair to the side and asks, "How are ye feeling, love?"

"Okay right now, but that could change at any moment." I am twelve weeks along with our third child. It had been a surprise, but one we are happy to have. "Another couple of weeks and me waistline will really start expandin'."

"And you'll still be sexy," he growls, kissing my cheek.

"Just so ye think so." He kisses my neck, dropping a hand to my hip.

"Isna that what keeps getting ye in trouble?" Evan

says, walking up, holding Audrey's hand.

"Aye, listen to you talking," Tavish says, grinning. "Just trying ta stay ahead of you two."

Audrey laughs. "Oh, I think ye had a head start on us from the beginning with twins. But we'll get there soon enough."

"Da!" Sarah cries, toddling up to Evan. "Bug!" She proudly opens her hand, sticky from cake icing, to reveal a small, partially smashed grasshopper. "Bug," she says again with a toothy smile.

"Uck!" Audrey covers her mouth. She is also in the early months of her second pregnancy and still suffering from bouts of morning sickness.

"Come on, darlin'," Evan says, picking her up. "Let's get ye cleaned up." He kisses Audrey and heads inside.

Audrey looks at me and shakes her head, pressing a hand against her stomach. "I'm looking forward to getting through this part. Good thing they are so worth it."

"Tell me about it."

Still wrapped in Tavish's arms, I stare out across the yard, taking in the faces of my family, and ponder all the amazing blessings in my life. Then I glance at Audrey's smiling profile. After years of feeling so far away from her and Yvonne, I am more grateful than I can say to have them in my life now. Audrey has had her share of sorrows and bouts of pain and grief, but God has compensated her by blessing her with all she could ever want and more. Her happiness has become mine, her joy, my joy.

It is definitely a good life.

About the Author

J. Adams has written books in different genres, but her main focus is inspirational interracial romance. She is a motivational speaker to both youth and adult audiences. In her spare time (when she has any) you can find her curled up with a good book and a healthy stash of orange Tic Tacs. She and her family reside in Utah.

Email: jewela40@gmail.com
Website: JewelAdams.com
Amazon Page: amazon.com/Jewel-Adams/e/B001TNK3GI/ref=ntt_dp_epwbk_0

www.ingramcontent.com/pod-product-compliance
Lightning Source LLC
Chambersburg PA
CBHW071343130626
46556CB00005B/1999